Ann Schweninger

Halloween Surprises

·BUTTON BROWN· ·MOTHER· ·BUTTERCUP· ·DAISY· ·FATHER·

Viking Kestrel

For Deborah Brodie and Barbara Hennessy

VIKING KESTREL

Viking Penguin Inc., 40 West 23rd Street, New York, New York 10010, U.S.A.
Penguin Books Ltd, Harmondsworth, Middlesex, England
Penguin Books Australia Ltd, Ringwood, Victoria, Australia
Penguin Books Canada Limited, 2801 John Street, Markham, Ontario, Canada L3R 1B4
Penguin Books (N.Z.) Ltd, 182–190 Wairau Road, Auckland 10, New Zealand

First Edition
First published in 1984 by Viking Penguin Inc.
Published simultaneously in Canada
Printed in Japan
1 2 3 4 5 88 87 86 85 84

Library of Congress Cataloging in Publication Data
Schweninger, Ann.   Halloween surprises.
Summary: After the Rabbit children have celebrated Halloween by
making costumes, carving jack-o'-lanterns, and going trick-or-treating,
their parents have one more surprise in store for them.
[1. Halloween—Fiction.   2. Rabbits—Fiction]   I. Title.
PZ7.S41263Hal   1984   [E]   83-27372
ISBN 0-670-35935-1

Costumes

YOU COULD BE A DEVIL.
OR A SKELETON.
I'LL BE A SCARECROW.
I'LL BE A MONSTER.

DAISY, WHAT ARE YOU GOING TO BE?

Jack-O-Lanterns

Trick or Treat